KU-160-498

To renew, find us online at:
https://capitadiscovery.co.uk/bromley

Please note: Items from the adult library may also accrue overdue charges when borrowed on children's tickets.

In partnership with
Bromley

CHISLEHURST
020 8467 1318

BETTER
the feel good place

10 Stories to Make a Difference is a collection of ten original illustrated stories for young readers, all inspired by the theme of *difference*. The collection features a mix of well-known and emerging writers and illustrators, giving a platform to untold stories and diverse new voices. Produced by Pop Up Projects, a non-profit, UK-based national children's literature development agency, 10 Stories celebrates Pop Up's 10th birthday in 2021. Proceeds from sales supports Pop Up's work in deprived schools, marginalised communities, and with talented writers and illustrators, especially from backgrounds that are under-represented in children's publishing. 10 Stories will be an annual publishing event, with a whole new collection planned for 2022.

Find out more at **www.pop-up.org.uk**

Sita Brahmachari is a writer of plays, short stories and novels for children and young adults including: *The River Whale, Where the River Runs Gold, When Secrets Set Sail, Corey's Rock* and *Worry Angels* (with Jane Ray), *Jasmine Skies, Kite Spirit* and *Red Leaves*. She won the Waterstones Children's Book Prize (2011) for her debut novel *Artichoke Hearts*, her novel *Tender Earth* was honoured by IBBY (2018), and she was a World Book Day 2021 author. Sita is an Amnesty International Ambassador and, working alongside Jane Ray, is writer-in-residence at the Islington Centre for Refugees and Migrants.

Jane Ray has illustrated over 50 picture books for children including *The Unicorn Prince* (with Saviour Pirotta), *Corey's Rock* (with Sita Brahmachari), *Hummingbird* (with Nicola Davies) and *The Tempest* (retold by Georghia Ellinas). She's been shortlisted for the Kate Greenaway Award six times, and was the IBBY UK Illustration Nominee for the Hans Christian Andersen Award in 2018. Working alongside Sita Brahmachari, Jane is also an artist-in-residence at the Islington Centre for Refugees and Migrants.

Edited by **Dylan Calder**, Pop Up Projects
Art directed by **Elorine Grant**, HarperCollins

Publisher **Dylan Calder**
Coordinator **Amanda Saakwa-Mante**
Designer **Txabi Jones**

Swallow's Kiss

Sita Brahmachari · Jane Ray

$\mathcal{I}$ place my finger to my lip
close my eyes and make a wish.

Mama says "It is not possible, it cannot be!"
there is no way I can remember the day
a bird dipped down into my pram
feather-wings fluttering over my lip
to leave its magic mark
but I DO remember.

In my forever memory-eye
swallows dart across the bright blue sky
glittering, twirling, floating, dipping, switching, diving
hovering over baby me
wings kissing my lip ever so gently
silvery swallow dust falling
to bring me, sing me, my name
in a thousand sweet-songed tongues
'Blessing'... Ble...sing... sing ... sing.

Like always Mama sings our Lingala lullaby
tonight I want to tell her
I'm not a baby like Ely anymore.

But Mama loves to sing like me
she always says
"Back home you, my Blessing, could sing
before you could talk
even before you could walk."

Some people's ears are closed to this city's sky-song
mine aren't
I hear the coo-coo of the pigeon
soft-throated sounds
alarm-clock geese and
long-throated swans.

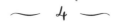

$\mathcal{M}$y ears are tuned
to the caged birds sitting
on the balcony below
with only the old woman
to sing to
I learn my scales
from these city birds
because this is my home.

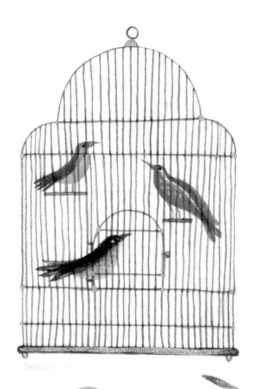

I wait till Mama's sung
her last sweet note
and I know the question
will make her groan
but I still have to ask
"How many sleeps
till Papa comes home?"

"Soon, Blessing, soon."
Mama touches her finger to her lip
I blow a kiss
"Good night, sweet swallow dreams."
"Night night, Mama."

School is long and I can't stop yawning
at break time I stand at the mesh to see if Mama waves
but the windows of Uncle Miral's cafe are all steamed up.

We have singing in the afternoon so time speeds up
then slows again in after-school club
like usual I'm the last to go home
I wait and wait for Miss Afia to walk me across the road
wishing Mama could come for me instead.

In Uncle Miral's cafe
Mama's cleaning tables
Ely strapped tight across her body
his podgy feet wriggling free.

"Hello sweet Blessing!"
Mama touches shadow moons of tired
under her eyes
when Miss Afia's gone she kisses me on the head
unstraps Ely and hands him over.

$\mathcal{I}$ sit in the back on sacks of rice
feeding Ely milk from his bottle
he falls asleep
suck-sucking
gently holding his silken head
I lower him on his dream pillow
and like a miracle he sleeps!

After juice and cake Mama hands me a rubbish bag
I don't mind helping
sometimes I find things to keep
things that people leave behind
Papa says "One person's rubbish is another's gold!"
at home I have a shelf for cafe finds
Uncle Miral and Mama tell me
if no one claims the left-behind treasure
I can keep it forever.

Today like every day Mama sweeps the crumbs out the door
Uncle Miral shoos the pigeons away
beckoning me to come see
points up at a flash of colour
testing me
'Para keeeeeeeeeeet!' I squawk
and they paint the sky green.

Mama turns the sign to closed
soon we can go home
"Come off that dirty floor my Blessing!"

"Mama, there's something under the table!"
I show her the bag and she smiles
"Eh! This Kobu print from home I have not seen for too long."
she holds it up "Light as feather…"

Ely starts to cry
Mama closes her eyes and deep deep sighs.

"'Wooooo!" I jump and drop it on the floor
a heart beats inside… maybe a mouse?
finger tips peep in to find a nest of rainbow wings
flit-flittering.

"Pleeeeeease Mamaaa! Can we take this home?"
she shakes her head
struggling to strap Ely to her
 "Blessing. I told NO."

My eyes tear up
Uncle Miral checks inside and winks at me
"Only a mish-mash of sparkly paper! No need of crying.
Borrow it but bring it back tomorrow."

Later I wait till Mama's sung Ely off to sleep
to show the bag again
Mama wants to see inside too!

I lift out a bright coloured bird
smells of glue we use at school
"Pretty!" I fly it above my head
"When Papa's here we can make some together."
"Can we Mama?" I bounce on the mattress. "Can we?"
Mama's phone rings in the other room
and I'm on my own.

Slowly one by one birds peck their way out of the bag

f l u t t e r u p
then come to settle on my
bed.

Trembly fingers unfold the paper
find squiggle words along the folds
written in alphabets I don't understand
like secret code
shimmering on golden wings
I spot the words
'Wish Birds'

But whose wishes?

My heart is a butterfly beating hard
fingers unfurl wings
and words
unfold.

Pomegranate رُمّان

Grandmother تِيتِي

I wish to see my DADDY AGAIN. HANI

Nest عُشّ

Who is Hani?

Tears burst from my eyes
because Hani's wish is the exact same as mine.

Build بنى

STAY يبقى

Orchard بستان

Moving يتنقّل

I place my fingers to my lip
close my eyes and make my wish
"Please can Papa come home tomorrow."

Home بيت

Family عيلة

Friend صاحب

Home وَطن

The globe light shines by my bed all night
I lie awake seeing with my imagination-eye
the long grey road my Papa drives
some nights I dream his lorry grows wings
to fly home above the jammed-up lines of traffic
looking down on all this earth
seeing what swallows see.

People walking long rubble-roads
like Mama did
tiny boats crossing giant seas
like Mama did
people like shoals of fish riding waves
like Mama did
when she came.

I hear the distant echo of papery song
feathery whispers
under my pillow.

Friend
صاحب

I close my eyes
imagining letters flying into the night
chasing through the park where blossom dances
over the church tower
the half-moon crescent of the mosque
the lines of houses and the shops
the school playground
Uncle Miral's cafe.

I'm a *Wish Bird* flying through confetti clouds
searching for Hani and the *Wish Bird*-makers
till swallows sumersault me into sleep.

Outside Uncle Miral's cafe pigeons peck the ground
he claps his hands looking to the sky
"No parakeets today!"
"There's some in here!" I say
handing him the bag of *Wish Birds*.

Hani's *Wish Bird* beats against my heart
guilt-wings prickle into me
what if someone comes to pick them up today
and I can't find a way to fly this home to Hani?

But what if it can bring my Papa home?

My not-sure feet dance this way that way
"Come on Blessing!" Mama calls from the pavement
waiting to cross me over the road.

At school Hani's *Wish Bird* lies
still and heavy under my vest
not whispering not fluttering not singing
and even though at the end of the day
I wish and wait
wish and wait
Papa does not come.

A woman walks out of Uncle Miral's cafe
across the road to the blue arch door
she wears a print wrap around her head like Mama's
beside her is a little boy
wide-eyes staring.

I trail along the mesh to be near
he's holding something close against his chest
the bag of *Wish Birds*!

"Hani?" I whisper.

Answering
his *Wish Bird* glows against my skin.

My trainers hit the pavement hard
sprinting to the blue door.

"Blessing! Wait for me! Where are you going?"
I hear Miss Afia call.

I push open the heavy door
entering
an echoing hall.

At the far end
a bright-clothed choir
their song is loud and deep and long
like voices flying together
through rough and stormy weather.

Then I see him
at a table
emptying out the bag of *Wish Birds*.

"Hani?"
he raises teary eyes
I run to him
and place the *Wish Bird* in his hand
crying out
he springs a hug on me.

"Welcome,"
a woman smiles
and asks my name
inviting me to sit at her
art table.

Hani shows me how to make a *Wish Bird*
cut, crayon, fold, paint, collage, decorate
he passes me glue
I stick feathers, ribbons, sequins
bead-buttons for the eyes.

At my shoulder
Wish Bird teacher's voice is feathery soft
"Beautiful, Blessing! If you've finished, on its wings
you can place your wishes."

What Hani writes
- 'Wish Friend?' -
makes me smile.

WISH FRIEND

Hani reaches up
touches his finger to my swallow lip
but I don't mind
the question in his eyes.

"Time to fly!"
teacher's arms grow into wings
eyes rise high
our Wish Birds soar
then louder than the choir
I hear
his shout
his voice
my Papa's at the door!

I fly to him
he twirls me round
crying for joy
spinning too fast
then slowly
slowing
settling.

Hani's kneeling on the floor
his Wish Bird lying quiet on his knee
choir sings a sour-sweet song
and my heart hurts for Hani.

Papa hears, sees, understands
gives Hani his hand
and helps my friend to stand.

"Papa! Papa! Look what we made!"
me and Hani race our *Wish Birds* round the hall
to the choir's loudening call.

I place my finger to my lip
and make another wish
for Mama and me to sing
together in this choir.

Hani runs at me
I bend down low
his hands wrap tight around my neck
like he never wants to let me go.

Wish Bird teacher comes to help
cuddles him close
dries his tears
and closes the blue door.

Across the road
happy pigeons coo-coo-coo
Mama stands with Uncle Miral
smiling, waving
holding Ely.

Wish Bird wings are fluttering fast
heart flies this way that way.

In my imagination-eye
a thousand shimmering swallows fill the sky.

I place my fingers to my lip
close my eyes and wish
harder than I've ever wished
for anyone
that one day
Hani's wish too
can come true.

Dedicated to the inspirational community at Islington Centre for Refugees and Migrants, with love and admiration (Sita & Jane)

Thank You!

The 10 Stories collection has been made possible through the generosity and love poured into these stories by our old friends and new, the writers and illustrators who all gave their wisdom and magic: Philip Ardagh, Avital Balwit, Jamie Beard, Sita Brahmachari, Eleanor Cullen, Danica Da Silva Pereira, Ria Dastidar, Alexis Deacon, Laura Dockrill, Jamila Gavin, Sahar Haghgoo, Jay Hulme, Daniel Ido, Krista M. Lambert, Jane Ray, Jacinta Read, Chris Riddell, David Roberts, Marcus Sedgwick, Anjali Tiwari. And through the kindness and devotion of the brilliant publishing editors, art directors and designers who volunteered their time to transform these great stories into even greater books: Emily Ball, Liz Bankes, Andrew Biscomb, Jane Buckley, Alice Curry, Holly Fulbrook, Lilly Gottwald, Elorine Grant, Libby Hamilton, Daisy Jellicoe, Txabi Jones, Ruth Knowles, Tiffany Leeson, Jacqui McDonough, Caroline Royds, Chloé Tartinville, Holly Tonks, Clare Whitston, Sean Williams. Huge gratitude to Matt Baxter and Lydia Fisher at Baxter & Bailey for donating their time to produce the 10 Stories brand, style and formats. If it wasn't for the 643 donors to our crowdfunding campaign, these books may never have made it to print - and we especially want to thank Rachel Denwood and Simon & Schuster, Sam Arthur and Nobrow, Michelle McLeod and Baillie Gifford, the CSR team at Linklaters LLP, Tim Bevan, Wolfgang Tillmans and all our former Board members for their generous support. Behind the scenes, the team and Board at Pop Up kept this great ship afloat through these most turbulent times, and we cannot thank them enough for always being part of the story no matter how hard the story gets.

Made possible by

 Baxter & Bailey HarperCollins *Children's Books*

This is a first edition. First published in Great Britain in 2021 by Pop Up Projects CIC 5 City Garden Row London N1 8DW. Text copyright © 2021 by Sita Brahmachari. Illustrations copyright © 2021 by Jane Ray. The rights of Sita Brahmachari and Jane Ray to be identified as the author and illustrator of this work have been asserted by them in accordance with the Copyrights, Designs and Patents Act, 1988. All rights reserved. Printed and bound in Poland by Ozgraf www.ozgraf.com.pl ISBN 978-1-8383-2350-9